THE OTHER SIDE OF INVISIBLE

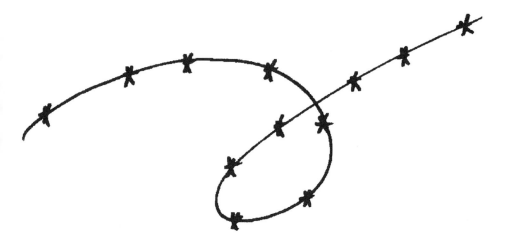

TREVOR ROMAIN

Published By:
BRIGHT BOOKS, INC.
2313 Lake Austin Boulevard, Austin TX 78703 (512) 499-4164

Cover Design: Bill Hanson

10 9 8 7 6 5 4 3 2 1

Library Of Congress Catalog Card Number 94-72241

ISBN 1-880092-17-4

In loving memory of my little friend

MEGAN STENTO
1984-1994

whose promising young life was cut short by childhood cancer.
Megan, during the last days of your life, I promised I would read
this book to you when it was published. And you said,
"Trevor, you'll have to read real loud if I'm in heaven."
To fulfill my promise to you, Megan, I will stand on the roof of
my house and read as loud as I can.
I love and miss you.

'Umuntu ngumuntu ngomnye'

'People are people through other people'

-Xhosa proverb

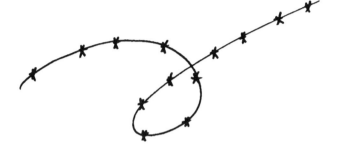

THE BEGINNING

Trevor Romain

Sipo walked toward the shed pulling his soapbox cart behind him.

Suddenly a strange feeling, like the arms of a cold wind, embraced his body. Although the day was hot, Sipo shivered, because he knew something was about to happen.

He wasn't wrong. Before he could take another step,

Albie Fenter rushed out from behind the shed and hurled himself at Sipo.

Sipo let go of his soapbox cart and ran, blindly.

But he was too slow and he knew it. He stopped running and covered his face, waiting for Albie to attack.

It never happened. He opened his eyes. Albie Fenter was triumphantly standing with his foot on Sipo's soapbox cart.

"Not the cart! Please!" pleaded Sipo. The cart had taken him two whole days to build. It was made from a crate he had found behind the farm house. It was the only thing besides his tattered clothes that he owned.

"But it's mine," said Albie Fenter, shrugging his shoulders.

"It's not!" said Sipo.

"It is!" yelled Albie. "I'm white. You're black."

This statement made Sipo angry. He charged. But he was much too small.

Albie rolled him over and pinned him to the ground.

"Blacks are slaves here in South Africa. Don't you know that, Sipo?"

"All I want to do is ride your cart," Albie said, getting up and brushing himself off.   "Besides, we're best friends. Remember our motto: United we stand..."

"And divided we fall," chuckled Sipo.

"Buddies forever," said Albie, slapping Sipo on the back.

"Buddies forever," said Sipo.

North Cliff was where all the farm kids went to ride their carts and roll old tires. There were two hills. The bottom slope was short and very steep, and all you had to do was stop before the fence. The upper slope was long and just as steep. There was a gate at the bottom, but there weren't many who could steer their carts down the top slope, through the narrow gate, and down the lower slope to the fence.

It was fast, and you had to lean way over at the gate. The only place on the whole slope where the cart could turn was a bump that made the cart take off. Chances were good that after the bump, the cart would hit either the huge thorn bush, the fence, or the shed.

"I'll swap you," said Albie.

"What for?" said Sipo.

"A ride for a comic book."

"What comic book?"

Albie removed a rolled up comic book from his jacket.

Sipo loved reading comic books.

Albie and Sipo walked up the slope together, Sipo

pulling his cart behind him. They talked and laughed as

they walked, their restless feet kicking at every small bush or stone on the path.

Once they reached the top, Albie Fenter sat in the soapbox cart and grinned. Suddenly he grabbed the comic book from Sipo and pushed off down the hill. The rickety crate bobbed up and down as it went. Sipo saw the cart hit a bump and lift into the air. Albie pushed his foot down hard just as he left the ground. He disappeared

through the gate and went out of sight behind the shed.

Sipo ran down the hill and through the gate. Albie was

sitting next to the shed door. He had pulled up exactly

right.

"Give me the comic book," said Sipo.

"But that was just a test ride. Take the cart back up

the hill for me and I'll test it again. If it passes this time

you can have the comic book."

"Why should I take it up the hill if you're going to ride

it down?" asked Sipo.

"Because you're black," said Albie.

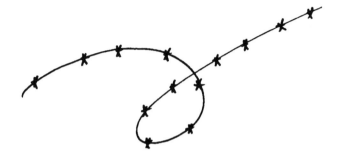

THE SPILL

At the top of the hill Albie pushed the cart hard and jumped into it. As he reached top speed, just before the hump, the right front wheel began to shudder. Even from where he was, Sipo could see the wheel buckling. Albie tried to brake, but couldn't; he lost control by putting both feet down. The wheel came off, the cart lifted into the air sideways, and Albie tumbled out of the box. Sipo heard the crunch and the smash and started running.

"What makes you think *that* was a soapbox cart?" said

Albie, angrily kicking at the splintered cart.

Albie Fenter took his comic book and walked towards

the beautiful farm house nestling beneath North Cliff.

Sipo left the remains of his cart piled against the shed

wall and set off for the comfort of his grandmother's hut.

The hut was also at the bottom of North Cliff almost a mile from the Fenter's farm house. It was a traditional Zulu hut, made of clay and red mud bricks. The roof was thatched with layer upon layer of dried grass.

Sipo's grandmother was an artist and a some-time witch doctor. A sangoma.

People came from far and wide to buy the wood

carvings his grandmother made. Many believed the carvings had good spirits which would bring them luck and healing.

Later, Sipo and his grandmother sat in the shadows sipping water from the barrel kept under the work bench. His grandmother threw the last drops of water into the fire, and wiped her wrinkled mouth.

"The chair is done," said his grandmother. "We can take it into town now."

Sipo sat on the carrier over the bicycle's back mudguard. He had one arm around his grandmother and the other entwined through the legs of the antique chair.

Sipo's grandmother was wonderful with her hands. She could do anything with wood. She often repaired furniture for the white people in the little town. She never looked at the wood she was working. Her hands seemed to find their own path and she hummed and chanted while she worked.

His grandmother pushed off and they began riding along the dirt road toward the small town in the distance. His grandmother always rode at the same pace, steadily, ignoring hills and valleys.

"Sit still, Sipo," she said. "You're wriggling like a Mopani worm."

Sipo had a tough time balancing on the back of the bicycle. The carrier was uncomfortable and there was nowhere for him to put his feet. He rested his face against his grandmother's back. The old rusty saddle squeaked as its tired springs spoke to the contours on the road.

Sipo waited with the bicycle while his grandmother took the chair into the back door of the antique store. A few minutes later she returned. The storekeeper, Mrs. Bekker, appeared behind her at the door. She handed her a few coins. Sipo's grandmother clapped her hands together traditionally and accepted the money with her head bowed.

The money would go toward buying a chicken for dinner. Mrs. Bekker reached into the door and brought out an old brown carton.

"A lot of these apples are over-ripe," she said softly. "But if you look carefully you'll find some nice ones."

Sipo's grandmother bowed her head once more.

Sipo couldn't understand why his wise, all-knowing grandmother looked so frail and afraid when she talked to white people.

It was dark when they reached home. Sipo's grandmother put the bicycle in the back room and collected a pile of wood for the dinner fire. Later, Sipo lit the oil lamp while his grandmother plucked the chicken and put the neatly cut pieces in a clay oven outside the door.

"While we wait," said Sipo's grandmother, "I will speak with the spirits of our ancestors."

She sat herself down on an old stool and took a swig from a bottle filled with homemade peach brandy. Sipo smiled. That night he would hear more stories about his grandmother's childhood.

"Tell me about Shaka Zulu," said Sipo.

"But I have told you the story more times than the summers of your life," chuckled his grandmother.

"I know," said Sipo, "but I love that story."

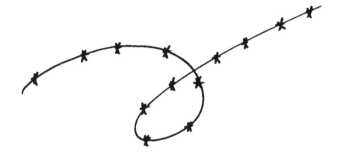

THE STORM

Just before dinner was ready, a storm swept in and blew against North Cliff. From his small window, Sipo watched the lightning illuminate the fields. He saw leaves flying and trees bending and writhing in the wind. He heard the corrugated iron roof of the shed crying under the strain. He looked over at the scarecrow in his grandmother's small vegetable garden.

The scarecrow seemed to be fighting against the wind. His flimsy broomstick arms gestured wildly as he argued with the storm. Sipo saw the storm try to push the scarecrow over, but the scarecrow fought back. Unfortunately, the scarecrow was no match for the storm. In an uncontrollable fit of temper, the cruel wind tore the shirt off the scarecrow's back and threw it against the barbed wire fence, ripping it to shreds. Sipo shivered.

"I wish we could be there and they could be here," he said, pointing at the Fenters' cozy home in the distance.

"They will always be there and you will always be here, Sipo."

"Why, grandmother?"

"Because they live on the other side of the invisible

fence" said his Grandmother. They are white and we are black, and that is the way of South Africa."

"One day I will change that," said Sipo, smiling. "I will become king and put a gate in the invisible fence."

Sipo's grandmother chuckled.

"You alone will never change this place, Sipo. Only the loss of much blood can do that now. But if by any chance you can do it without a war, run and tell me right away."

Sipo's grandmother opened the clay oven door and pulled out the chicken.

After dinner Sipo sat on the sill and gazed out of the window. His grandmother kept on looking at him and shaking her head. She was laughing.

"So you think you can change the world," said his grandmother, getting ready for bed. "It will take more than a storm like this to move a mountain," she said, pulling the covers over her old frame.

Sipo thought about his mother and father. He had seen them only a few times in the four years he'd been living on the farm with his grandmother. They had sent Sipo away from the city after a violent riot in the township where he lived.

He trembled as he thought about the men fighting in the field behind his house in Sharpeville. He remembered the policemen with big dogs chasing the men through the clouds of tear gas, which wafted across the field and into his home where it hurt his eyes.

Sipo went to bed and dreamed he had become the king of all South Africa. He dreamed he helped the black people make peace with each other and that Albie Fenter had become his servant.

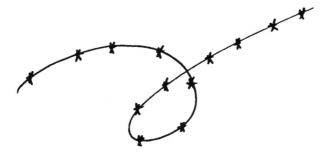

THE CART

The next morning was Sunday. With no work in the fields, Sipo's grandmother got some wood from the old shed behind the hut and set two lengths on the work-bench. She sorted through the other wood pieces on the floor and marked them all the same length with a ruler and a pencil.

Then she began to work.

She cut the wood with an old saw. She started each cut by drawing the saw backwards, towards herself. Then she moved fast, cutting dead true, her old hand and thumb clamping the wood to the bench.

After cutting, she fixed the two longest pieces of wood a distance apart, parallel to each other; then she nailed a length of different wood across the bottom. Behind it she put another; and so she went on. She worked quickly.

The nails went into the wood without bending.

In the tool shed at the farmhouse, Albie Fenter looked

at the soapbox cart he'd just completed.

His cart was made from expensive oak struts. His

father had helped him mount a brand new chrome swivel

on the front axle and a nylon sash on the beam so he could steer her well.

She was a beauty. He called her Lightning.

He left his father's tools lying on the shed floor and set off down the path towards North Cliff.

Sipo's grandmother turned the whole frame over,

took four small wheels and fitted them on the frame. She

took a screw, held it in one of the holes and drove it home.

Her grip on the screw driver made her black knuckles

white.

When his grandmother stood back, Sipo saw a brand

new cart.

"Ha," said his grandmother. "I can feel the spirit of Africa in this cart. It is the magic of the wood from the Geel Hout tree. I can see the wheels moving, never stopping."

She touched the wheels with her rough hands and smiled.

"You must keep the wheels oiled," she said,

"because the sand will tighten them up."

She got up and opened a box near her chair. It was full of wire and rope. She chose a length of rope, threaded it through the eyes she had cut, knotted the ends, and the cart was complete.

She stood back and smiled.

"Now take it to North Cliff and give it a good run.

"My bones ache. I think I'll take a nice quiet rest while you're gone."

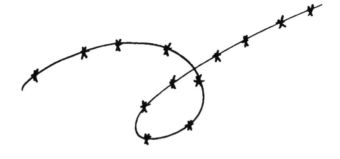

THE RACE

Sipo walked down the path from the hut. The cart jerked a little at first and left oil stains on the dirt road.

He pulled the cart up North Cliff's bottom slope. It was heavy, but the rope didn't cut. The cart was strong and well balanced and carried a lot of its own weight.

As Sipo was about to pull the cart through the gate, he heard a flurried rattle approaching. Suddenly there was a gasp in the air and a cart appeared from behind the shed. The rider skidded across the sand, over the bump and through the gate.

"Yahoo!"

It was Albie Fenter.

"Where'd you get *that* from?" asked Albie.

"My grandmother," said Sipo. "She made it for me.

Where'd you get yours?"

"I made it myself, stupid. Without any help. Besides, your grandmother is a witch. What does she know about carts?"

"She put a spirit in my cart," said Sipo. "And besides, my grandmother is not a witch. She's a witch doctor. A sangoma."

They looked each other's carts over and then looked at the slope.

"Let's have a race," said Albie. "I bet my cart's a lot faster than your trash heap. Mine's made from real oak."

"I'll still lose, even if I win," said Sipo. "You'll take my cart."

"No," said Albie, " the winner gets a prize. A big prize."

"What?" asked Sipo.

"You decide."

"You won't like what I choose, Albie."

"Yes I will, Sipo."

"Okay," said Sipo. "The winner gets to be the king of South Africa."

"That's fine with me," said Albie. "I'll make a good king

and you'll make a good servant."

The slope was waiting. Only boys with great courage raced from that height.

Sipo looked down the hill and tugged his cart around.

"Go!" shouted Albie as soon as Sipo's cart was level with his own.

Sipo sat astride the cart. His heels braced. He let out the rope, lay back and eased the cart forward. He felt the speed and rhythm of the hill. Albie was way ahead of him yelling madly into the air as he went.

Sipo's cart found its own course. The steering moved in his hands and arms and then his shoulders and then he was going so fast he passed Albie's cart with ease.

Albie kicked out at him. But it was too late.

The thorn trees were a blur as he passed. He saw the bump and the narrow gate but felt no fear. He took in more rope, gripped hard and closed his eyes. It took an eternity, but the cart wheels landed without shock.

Behind him he heard Albie's shoes scrape across the ground for balance. Sipo pulled on the rope and cocked his head to the right. His weight brought him forward and

he moved comfortably through the gate. He dug his heels

into the dirt, swung the cart hard to the right and slid to

a dusty stop mere inches from the shed door.

Sipo whipped his head around to get a better look at

the gate. Albie Fenter's cart hit the bump and hung in the

air for the longest time. Sipo heard the wood split and

crack; and the cart and Albie Fenter tumbled across the path in slow motion.

"I won," yelled Sipo. "I am the king!"

"No way," shouted Albie, rubbing his bruised elbow.

Sipo ran home ignoring Albie's anger.

"Grandma, Grandma," yelled Sipo as he neared the hut.

He pulled the cart up and left it by the door. He opened

the door. The room was empty but the lamp was lit.

Sipo heard the rocking chair squeaking in the work-room. He smiled.

"I changed it all, Grandmother," he yelled, rushing into the room.

Albie's father was sitting in his grandmother's chair. Sipo stopped.

"Where's my Grandmother?"

"She's in her room, Sipo," said Albie's father, "but she is very ill."

"I need to speak to her," said Sipo. "It's urgent."

"She might not hear you," said Albie's father gently. "We are waiting for the ambulance to come from Greytown."

"I must speak with her," urged Sipo.

"Go to her," said Albie's father. "But just for a minute"

Sipo entered his grandmother's room. The shades were pulled. It was dark except for the light of a single candle. The old lady was lying peacefully on the hand-made wooden bed. Her breathing was very shallow. Sipo took his grandmother's hand in his own.

"Grandmother," he whispered.

There was no reply.

"Grandmother. I am the king. Now I have the power to break down the invisible fence."

Still there was no reply.

Sipo reached over and kissed his grandmother on the cheek.

He stood up and was about to leave the room when his grandmother spoke.

"Step carefully, Sipo," whispered his grandmother, "because even an invisible fence can be made from barbed wire."

She sighed and closed her eyes. Sipo knew they would never open again.

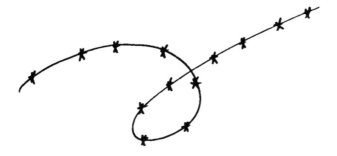

THE WAITING SLOPE

Sipo rushed from the house. The cart pulled easily

as he ran all the way up to the highest part of North Cliff.

The highest part where no one dared ride from.

There wasn't a soul on North Cliff.

Sipo heeled himself forward. The cart moved gently,

surely, sensitive to the touch. She steered beautifully. He

felt the hill through the cart, as if he and the hill were one.

There were no jolts. The wheels glided over the ruts and ran true to the waiting slope.

Albie was waiting for Sipo at the bottom of the hill. He stepped forward as the cart pulled up in front of the shed.

"This belongs to you," he said, handing Sipo the comic book.

They both walked silently back toward North Cliff. As they moved through the gate, young Sipo Keswa hung back a step and let Albie Fenter have it across the top of the head with the rolled up comic book.

❧

23 years later, on April 27, 1994, the first all race election took place in South Africa.

Both Sipo Keswa and Albie Fenter voted.

During the following month Nelson Mandela became the first black President of the new South Africa.

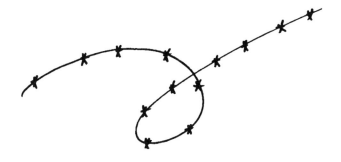

THE CALL

The call came during a heavy thunderstorm. Sipo was having a quiet dinner with his wife and young daughter when the phone rang.

"I have something that belongs to you," said a voice on the phone.

"I beg your pardon," replied Sipo. A long day in court had tired him out and he wasn't in the mood for crank calls.

"Is this Sipo Keswa?" asked the voice. "The best lawyer in town?"

Sipo's back stiffened. The police had warned him that some of the criminals he had put behind bars might try to get even with him when they were released. He was about to put the receiver down when the voice spoke again.

"Sipo, I have a wooden soapbox cart that belongs to you."

Sipo gasped.

"My dad died recently and I was cleaning out the old shed. Although it's twenty three years old, your cart is still in good shape. I thought you might want it back."

"Albie Fenter!" yelled Sipo. "It's been years. How on

earth are you?"

"Well, I'm in a little trouble," said Albie.

"How so?" asked Sipo.

"The bank is trying to take the farm away from us."

"No," mumbled Sipo.

"Yes," said Albie, sadly. "But farming isn't what it used to be. We're struggling. My father didn't leave a will and they want to take the farm to pay down his debt. I can work it all out but I just need time. And a little help."

"But North Cliff has been in your family for four generations," said Sipo.

"Yes," said Albie, in the same mournful tone. "I could use your help to keep it that way, Sipo. Unfortunately

I have no money..."

"That's okay. We can work out a trade," said Sipo,

grinning. "Got any comic books?"

ABOUT **THE AUTHOR**

Trevor Romain was born in South Africa and lived in Johannesburg until he was 28. He moved to the United States in the late eighties to pursue his writing career.

The author of 10 children's books, Mr. Romain lives with his wife Amiel in Austin, Texas.

Trevor spends a lot of his time with children who have cancer and is currently writing about his experiences with these children.

OTHER BOOKS BY **TREVOR ROMAIN**

The Big Cheese

The Little People's Guide To The Big World I

The Little People's Guide To The Big World II

The Keeper Of The Dreams

The Boy Who Swallowed A Rainbow

Under The Big Sky

COMING **SOON**

Where The Moonbeams Waltz

How Can You Go To Bed With An Elephant In Your Head?

There's A Lady In The Attic And I Don't Like Her Face!